T0354582

Why James Likes to go to School!

VIBHA JAYAN

Why James Likes to go to school!

BY VIBHA JAYAN

My life is wonderful because my mom and dad encouraged me to go to school and helped me learn about new things. I am forever thankful for their efforts.

Vibha Jayan

It was a nice sunny day. Mama dressed up James for the school, but James did not like to go to school.

All his friends went to school. Instead of going to school, James decided he would find a friend to play with all day.

While walking, he saw a squirrel.

He asked the squirrel," Dear squirrel, can we play together?"

Squirrel wondered why James was not in school. She said,
"Sorry, dear James. Winter is coming. I have to collect
pine nuts otherwise I will not have any food for the winter."
She put a few pine nuts in her mouth and ran to hide it.

On the way James met a cute little bird
with some twigs in her beak.

He smiled and asked the bird. "Hey mama bird, Will you be my friend and play with me?" Mama Bird was surprised to see that James was not in school. She said, "Dear, I don't have time. I have to build my nest for the winter otherwise my little ones and I will freeze in the cold."

James felt sad, but he still hoped to find a new friend. Suddenly he saw leaf cutter ants walking in a line and carrying green leaves on their heads. He thought ants were having too much fun. Maybe they will play with him.

He asked the ants " Can I play with you all?" Ant said,
"No sir, we are not playing. We are building
our nest with these leaves. We are enjoying
ourselves while working. Maybe you should too.
Go back to your school and enjoy learning."

James was disappointed. He still hoped to find someone who was free and would be willing to play with him. Finally, he met a caterpillar.

He asked the caterpillar, "Oh! Dear caterpillar, please, can you play with me? I don't want to go to school." Caterpillar laughed at James and said," I am surprised James that you don't want to learn about new things by going to school. Right now, I have to build my cocoon so that I can become a beautiful butterfly and fly around freely. If you do not want to be ignorant, then go to school and learn about new things."

Now James realized that everyone enjoyed
doing what they were supposed to do.
Maybe he was doing something wrong.

James was tired of walking around trying to find a friend. Suddenly he saw his friend Niam. Niam's dad was driving him to school.

Niam's dad stopped the car. Niam opened the window and shouted loudly to James. "James, my friend, hop in. Let's go to school together." James was very happy to see Niam.

He was looking for a friend the whole day,
while all his friends were in school.

From that day onwards James decided he will go to school, play with his friends and learn about new things.

Copyright © 2024 Vibha Jayan.

All rights reserved. No part of this book may be used or reproduced by any means, graphic, electronic, or mechanical, including photocopying, recording, taping or by any information storage retrieval system without the written permission of the author except in the case of brief quotations embodied in critical articles and reviews.

This is a work of fiction. All of the characters, names, incidents, organizations, and dialogue in this novel are either the products of the author's imagination or are used fictitiously.

Archway Publishing books may be ordered through booksellers or by contacting:

Archway Publishing
1663 Liberty Drive
Bloomington, IN 47403
www.archwaypublishing.com
844-669-3957

Because of the dynamic nature of the Internet, any web addresses or links contained in this book may have changed since publication and may no longer be valid. The views expressed in this work are solely those of the author and do not necessarily reflect the views of the publisher, and the publisher hereby disclaims any responsibility for them.

ISBN: 978-1-6657-6336-3 (sc)
ISBN: 978-1-6657-6335-6 (hc)
ISBN: 978-1-6657-6337-0 (e)

Library of Congress Control Number: 2024915124

Print information available on the last page.

Archway Publishing rev. date: 07/27/2024